Yellow Wellies

Yellow Wellies

Jan Godfrey

Illustrated by Branwen Thomas

Scripture Union

By the same author

Oliver and the Big Green Snake – Read to Me series

© Jan Godfrey 1996

First published 1996

Scripture Union, 207–209 Queensway,
Bletchley, Milton Keynes, MK2 2EB, England.

ISBN 1 85999 051 7

British Library Cataloguing-in-Publication Data.
A catalogue record of this book is available from the British
Library.

Printed and bound in Great Britain by Cox & Wyman Ltd,
Reading.

Contents

For Elizabeth

At the pond

Adam went to the pond with his school class and his teacher, Miss Johnson. They took fishing nets and jam-jars and worksheets and pencils because ponds are very interesting places.

It was a warm, sunny day at the beginning of the summer term. There were snails and tadpoles and frogs to look for. There were waterlilies growing on top of the pond, and flowers and tall plants round the edge.

Miss Johnson sorted the children into groups. Some of them went off to draw the pond. Some of them went to look at the plants. Some of them went to see if they could find any tadpoles or tiny frogs. Adam's group went fishing.

'Be careful,' warned Miss Johnson. 'It's a bit muddy at the edge.'

'There's a stickleback!' said Adam, pointing excitedly to a little fish that was darting in and out of the weeds. He dragged his net through the water but the stickleback disappeared underneath it.

'Bother, it's gone,' said Adam. He had another go. This time the stickleback swam right in, but just as Adam lifted his net, it swam out again.

'Bother BOTHER,' said Adam, feeling quite cross. 'They always get away.'

But he wasn't cross for long. The park was lovely and sunny and nicer than his garden at home. Dad was digging it up for something and it seemed rather small and dull and full of rubble and not much grass.

Adam's friend Parminder came to help, and Sheena and Mark and Carly crowded round as well. But nobody could catch that stickleback. Then Adam put down his net and tried feeling for it with his hands. The water was pleasant and cool but all he could feel was the tangled pondweed.

'Let's try with ALL our nets at once,' suggested Mark. 'Look! There's the stickleback again!'

The nets clattered together and caught in the weed and the children started to slither about in the mud.

'Ohhh ...!' shouted Parminder, clutching at Adam who grabbed Carly, who fell against Sheena, who nearly knocked Mark over in the mud. Somehow, they all found themselves slithering nearer the water. Carly and Adam and Parminder were getting very wet indeed.

Miss Johnson came over to see what was happening, and was rather cross.

'You'd better come right away from the pond for a while,' she said. 'Adam and Carly and Parminder, your feet are soaking wet. You'd better take off your shoes and socks and let them dry in the sun. Come over to me when you're ready for some spare trainers to wear.'

The rest of the group went off with Miss Johnson to the other side of the pond. While she was busy telling them what to do next, Carly had an idea.

'We could use our nets to catch butterflies while our shoes and socks get dry,' she said to Adam. 'Just for a minute. Miss Johnson will be pleased.'

They ran about and danced on the warm grass, waving their nets. There were one or two butterflies but they didn't want to fly into Adam and Carly's nets. Then Carly said, 'Ooh, Adam, look!'

'What are you two doing now?' called Miss Johnson, turning round. 'Come over here at once for your shoes.'

'But I saw something beautiful!' said Carly. 'Something blue and green and it had wings and – '

'It looked like a helicopter!' said Adam. 'Look – there it goes again!'

'I like that helicopter,' said Parminder.

'That's a dragonfly, not a helicopter,' laughed Miss Johnson, as all the class gathered round to look.

The dragonfly had a blue-green body and transparent wings. The colours seemed to change as it flew and zoomed past them in the sunshine and skimmed the pond, hovering for a moment, then darting on past them again.

'That's beautiful!' said Carly.

'They like the sunshine,' said Miss Johnson. 'That's when they like to go flying and looking for insects.'

'I've never seen one in my garden,' said Sheena.

'Perhaps you haven't a pond in your garden,' said Miss Johnson. 'Dragonflies like ponds. They always live near pond water.'

'I would like a pond in my garden,' said Parminder. 'Then I could look for dragonflies.'

'So would I,' said Adam, longingly.

Soon the morning at the pond was over and it was time to go back to school.

'Our shoes and socks are dry again,' said Carly and Adam. 'But the grass felt nice and tickly under our bare feet.'

Back in the classroom, Miss Johnson's class was busy for the rest of the week. The children all showed and told each other what they had found and seen and done at the pond. There were pictures of flowers and waterlilies on the walls, and jam-jars with some tadpoles on the shelves. All the children had written about everything that they'd seen or noticed or watched or found. They all talked about their visit.

'I found a frog,' said Ryan.

'I found some tadpoles,' said Emma. 'They were wriggly.'

'I saw a waterlily,' said Sunao. 'It was very beautiful. I have seen them in my country too, in Japan.'

'We nearly caught a butterfly in our fishing nets,' said Adam, 'but it flew away.'

'I expect the butterfly was much happier not being caught in your fishing net,' said Miss Johnson. 'They are very delicate and it would have damaged itself. It will be much happier flying where it wants in the sunshine.'

'And we saw a beautiful, beautiful dragonfly,' said Parminder. 'We thought it was a helicopter!'

Then Miss Johnson's class made a huge picture together of the pond. Everyone put something on the picture or painted part of it. There were lots of tadpoles and butterflies and flowers, and Carly and Parminder and Adam made giant dragonflies out of silver foil and coloured cellophane paper. The dragonflies hung from the ceiling and looked as if they were hovering over the picture. Miss Johnson was so pleased with it that it was put in the school hall where the children had assembly together every morning.

'It will be nice to look at when we sing our songs to God,' said Miss Johnson. 'It will remind us what a beautiful world God has made with so many different places and homes for all the creatures.'

At assembly news-time Adam was excited and fidgety. He kept whispering to Parminder and Carly. Then at last it was his turn! He jumped up and said loudly:

'I know now what my dad's making in the garden! He's building a little pond!'

Adam felt happy. He hoped that Parminder and Carly and Mark and Sheena and all his friends would come to tea one day, and they'd all look for dragonflies.

PRAYER

Thank you God, for insects and frogs and plants that live near ponds. It's really interesting learning all about them and how to treat them carefully. You have made them all so perfectly, and they are beautiful and wonderful. *Amen*

Amanda in the middle

Once upon a time there was a very large family whose name was Smith. There were a great many brothers and sisters and cousins. There was Mr Smith and Mrs Smith and Grandma Smith and Grandpa Smith. There was Aunty Smith and Uncle Smith. There was Sally Smith, who was twelve years old, and there was Stephen Smith, who was ten years old, and there was Sarah Smith, who was eight years old. They were the Big Smiths. Then there came Ben Smith and Bianca Smith who were both four and were twins, and last of all there was Baby Smith who was no years at all yet, just a little bit older than nothing. They were the Little Smiths.

And right in the middle was Amanda Smith!

Amanda was six. The family all said things like this:

'Amanda, give me a hand with the baby,' Mum would say. 'There's a dear. Just rock the pram for a moment, will you – the big ones are too busy and the little ones are too little.'

Or Dad would say, 'Amanda, run and get my book for me will you, there's a good girl. There's nobody else around.'

Or Grandpa Smith would say, 'Just pass my glasses will you, Amanda dear,' when the Big Smiths were busy with an important game.

Or Grandma Smith would say, 'Just get my slippers will you, Amanda dear,' when the Little Smiths were nowhere to be seen.

Or Aunty Smith would say, 'Well, I think you're too young for that, Amanda, wait until you're a bit older.'

Or Uncle Smith would say, 'Now Amanda, you're a bit old for that, aren't you?'

Or Baby Smith would say, 'Waaaaaaaaaaaaah!!!' and Amanda would cuddle him because she did love him very much indeed.

But it was a nuisance being in the middle!

The Big Smiths would say, 'Oh no, Amanda, you're not big enough for our game. Go and play with the little ones.'

Or the Little Smiths would say, 'Go away, Amanda, it's OUR game. You're too big!'

Now Amanda was on the whole an amiable, good-tempered little girl and she did like her brothers and sisters and all the rest of her family, but she was tired of being Amanda-in-the-Middle.

'I'm not big enough and I'm not small enough and I'm not old enough and I'm not young enough,' thought Amanda. 'I must do something about it.'

And this is what Amanda did:

On Sunday, Amanda went to church with all the family, who took up two rows of seats. While everyone was singing hymns and songs and saying prayers, Amanda took the opportunity to have a little private whisper in God's ear. She told God all about being in the middle of the family and how she wasn't big

enough and she wasn't little enough and would he do something about it please.

On Monday, Amanda walked round the house with her arms stretched in the air to make herself look bigger. She felt taller at once. But nobody took any notice.

On Tuesday, Amanda raided the dressing-up box. She dressed up in high heels and a dress of Mum's and put a hat with feathers on her head. But everybody was far to busy to even look at Amanda and see how grown up she'd suddenly become.

On Wednesday, Amanda stood on a chair. But she soon found that boring.

On Thursday, it was the day to start being little. Amanda curled up as small she could in the armchair. Nobody saw her, except the cat, who sat on her.

On Friday, she climbed into Baby Smith's cot, but nobody came in to see her, so she climbed out again.

And then, on Saturday, the Great Big Smiths came to stay.

Great Grandpa Smith was very old. He had a long beard and twinkly eyes and gnarled hands and he wore spectacles.

Great Grandma Smith was very old too. She wore a purple cardigan and a locket and chain. She looked rather stern and she wore her hair in a bun.

They all sat down to tea. Amanda sat in the 'excuse-me' seat which is the unfortunate place to be where you find everyone is passing things round you and in front of you and behind you saying 'excuse me' all the time.

Everyone talked at the tops of their voices all through the meal except Great Grandma Smith and Great Grandpa Smith who sat very silently and straight.

'I want an egg sandwich, please,' said Amanda, but nobody heard.

The Big Smiths were all telling jokes and silly stories. The Little Smiths were arguing about the last chipolata sausage and Baby Smith was blowing bubbles in his milk. Suddenly, Amanda forgot to be Amanda-in-the-Middle. She forgot that the Great Big Smiths, who were really very old and wise, had come to tea. She stood on her chair and she shouted VERY loudly, just like you might do if you were very BIG or very LITTLE.

'Please will someone pass me an egg sandwich!'

And everyone was so surprised – that they did! Everybody did – all at once, so that Amanda had a great many egg sandwiches on her plate. And the Great Big Smiths laughed and laughed and said, 'Amanda, come and sit between us and tell us what you've been doing.'

And Amanda did. What she told them was all about being Amanda-in-the-Middle. The Great Big Smiths didn't laugh but they listened very carefully and explained that the middle was a very special place to be, and that everybody in the world was as special as everybody else.

After tea, the children all went out into the garden and played Pig-in-the-Middle with Amanda's ball.

The ball went up into the tree and stuck in the branches. Amanda scrambled after it because the Big Smiths didn't want to get their new trainers and best skirts dirty and spoiled, and the Little Smiths were too little to reach. Amanda perched high up in the tree and threw the ball down as hard as she could.

And everyone said: 'Thank you, Amanda! You were JUST the right size! Great! Come and play with us!'

Amanda joined in and they all ran about all over the garden.

Then they went indoors, and Great Grandma Smith showed Amanda how to cut out a row of paper dolls. That was fun, and Great Grandma said:

'Look how special each one is, Amanda.'

'Why, yes,' said Amanda. 'They're all important. They all hold each other together!'

The next day was Sunday again and all Amanda's family went to church and sat in two rows of seats again.

'Thank you God,' whispered Amanda in God's ear. Somehow she knew that it didn't matter to God what size or shape or age you were. God loved you just the same, and you were just as important whether you were big, or little, or somewhere in the middle.

Thank you God, for families, for mums and dads and brothers and sisters and cousins. We know that you were part of a family when you lived on earth, and that you had brothers and sisters too. Help us to learn to live together happily, and to remember that however big or small we are, we are all very, very special. *Amen*

People

Aunty Pat wears a hat;
Uncle Paul is very tall.

Baby Andrew sometimes cries;
My friend Rakhi has brown eyes.

Cousin Julie lives in France –
You should see her sing and dance.

Next-door Rosa goes to Spain;
There and back by aeroplane.

Grandma's short and Grandpa's thin;
My teacher helps with everything.

Mum and Dad just love me a lot –
Then there's me – I nearly forgot!

So many people, big and small,
And I know God loves them all.

The barbecue picnic

James and Joanna were staying at Grandad and Grandma's house. It was a hot, sunny day.

'Let's have a barbecue at lunch-time,' said Grandma.

'In the back garden,' said Grandad.

'A real barbecue picnic!' said Joanna excitedly.

'I'm hungry already!' said James.

James and Joanna helped to get everything ready for the barbecue. They were busy all the morning sorting out charcoal for the fire, and sausages and baked beans and onions and chicken and burgers and bread rolls and lemonade.

They were all so busy that nobody noticed a little white cloud appearing in the blue sky. Another and another appeared ... getting more and more grey ... until by lunch-time, just as Grandad was lighting the barbecue, the sky had become quite dark.

And then – splash! A drop of rain sizzled on the fire, then there was a rumble of thunder and a flash of lightning, and it started pouring with rain. It began to feel much colder.

'Quickly, we must take everything indoors,' said Grandma, and they gathered everything up and ran inside out of the rain.

'Bread and cheese for lunch after all,' teased Grandad.

James and Joanna were terribly disappointed.

'We were so looking forward to the barbecue,' said Joanna sadly.

'Stupid old rain spoiling everything,' grumbled James. It was already the worst barbecue ever.

'Spoiled? Who said anything about spoiled?' said Grandad.

'No picnic? Who said there wouldn't be a picnic?' said Grandma. 'We'll have our barbecue picnic – indoors!'

'We can't have a barbecue indoors!' said James and Joanna together.

'Can't we?' said Grandma. 'Just you wait!'

'Can't we?' said Grandad. 'Just you see!'

Soon there was a wonderful smell of frying onions and sausages and burgers wafting from the kitchen cooker. Grandad wore his striped cook's apron, and James and Joanna helped count out the sausages and stir the baked beans. Then they went into the living room, and stared.

'Whatever are you doing, Grandma?' said James and Joanna together.

'Getting ready for our indoor picnic,' said Grandma.

She was drawing the living-room curtains and arranging cushions and a rug on the floor. It was really dark now, like a secret little world indoors. The children could hear the stormy rain still pouring down outside, but it didn't seem to matter quite so much.

'Now, turn on the sun, will you, James,' said Grandma, pointing to the ceiling light, and James, surprised, obeyed.

'Thank you,' said Grandma. 'And Joanna – we need some trees and hedges. Don't fall over the cushions, they're bushes. Bring over those pot plants, and the vase of flowers ... that's right, put them down to grow on the green carpet – it's lovely soft grass.'

The indoor barbecue was wonderful. Never mind the rain! James and Joanna and Grandad and Grandma ate their sausages and burgers and beans and bread rolls off paper plates, and drank lemonade out of paper cups. They ate and ate but there were still some little sausages left over.

Then they went on pretending. They pretended that they were having their picnic right out in the countryside.

'I can see a cow in that field over there,' said Grandad, pointing at a picture on the wall.

'And look at those birds!' said Grandma, looking at some china ducks that she kept on the wall and looked as if they were flying.

'I can see the sea now,' giggled Joanna, joining in this funny game. She pointed at the blue curtains. Pretending was fun. You could be anywhere you wanted!

'Can we have an ice-cream?' said James plaintively, and went out to the refrigerator.

When he came back he said,

'It's nearly stopped raining!'

But nobody wanted to go outdoors yet. The indoor picnic was far too much fun.

They ate their ice-cream, and Grandma read stories to James and Joanna. Then Grandad pretended he was a horse who'd come to join their picnic, and the children climbed on his back and rode on him. Then they played music and danced picnic dances all over the grassy carpet.

Then there was a ring at the door bell.

It was Mrs Plucknett from next door. She'd come to borrow a packet of tea – and she stayed and joined in the barbecue picnic.

Then there was another ring at the door bell.

It was Mr Plucknett from next door, wondering where Mrs Plucknett had got to with the packet of tea – and he stayed and joined in the barbecue picnic.

Then there were six rings at the front door bell.

This time it was all the little Plucknetts from next door wondering where Mum and Dad were – and they stayed and joined in the barbecue picnic.

There was lots of noise and fun and the little Plucknetts ate up all the little left-over sausages.

At last, the indoor picnic was over. The rain really had stopped, and there was even a watery sun shining in the garden. The Plucknetts all went home with lots of goodbyes and their packet of tea.

'That was a lovely, lovely picnic,' said Joanna, hugging Grandma.

'That was a great barbecue,' said James, holding Grandad's hand.

Joanna and James thought that grandmas and grandads were very special. Somehow, today they'd changed everything from being very disappointing into a wonderful game and a wonderful picnic.

It had been the best barbecue ever!

PRAYER

Thank you, God, for grandmas and grandads, and aunties and uncles. They're kind and they love us and they look after us sometimes. Thank you for the special way they read us stories, and have good ideas and play wonderful games. *Amen*

The very big apple

'I am pretty today,' said Donna-Jane, looking at herself in the mirror when she was ready to go to Gary Gribble's birthday party.

She didn't like Gary Gribble that much, but she did love parties.

'I am wearing my best hair ribbons,' said Donna-Jane.

'My hair is nice and curly.

'My party dress is lovely.

'My socks are clean and my shoes are new.

'My face is beautiful.

'I have a secret present all wrapped up in shiny paper.

'I am all ready to go to Gary Gribble's birthday party.'

'Hurry up,' said Donna-Jane's mother.

Donna-Jane pouted. She didn't want to hurry.

She liked looking at herself in the mirror.

But she ran downstairs.

She fell over the cat and banged her knee.

That made her feel annoyed.

So she smacked the cat.

'Give us a kiss goodbye,' said Donna-Jane's father.

But there wasn't time.

Donna-Jane slammed the door crossly.

The door caught her hair ribbon and pulled it off.

Donna-Jane stamped her foot.

'Mind the puddle,' said Donna-Jane's mother.

But it was too late.

Donna-Jane had a wet shoe.

The hem of her dress was splashed.

She stamped the other foot again, furiously.

Now the other foot was wet, too.

And muddy.

Donna-Jane began to cry.

She rubbed her eyes and made her face dirty.

'Oh Donna-Jane,' said Donna-Jane's mother.

'Whatever shall we do with you? Your party clothes are spoiled.

'But hurry along, or we shall never get to Gary Gribble's birthday party.'

On the way they met kind old Mr Joe.

'You look pretty today, Donna-Jane,' said kind old Mr Joe.

'And you have a secret present all wrapped up in shiny paper.

'You must be going to Gary Gribble's birthday party. But isn't it– ?'

Donna-Jane muttered and mumbled and moped.

She thought old Mr Joe looked WRINKLED.

Donna-Jane pulled a RUDE face.

'I am cross with you,' said Donna-Jane's mother.

Further on their way they met nice chatty Mrs Molly.

'You look pretty today,' said nice chatty Mrs Molly.

'And you have a secret present all wrapped up in shiny paper.

'You must be going to Gary Gribble's birthday party.

But I thought – '

Donna-Jane sniffed and snivelled and scowled.

She thought chatty Mrs Molly talked TOO MUCH.

Donna-Jane put her tongue RIGHT out.

'I am not pleased with you,' said Donna-Jane's mother.

At last, they reached Gary Gribble's birthday party.

But it wasn't Gary Gribble's birthday party.

'There's no party today,' said Gary Gribble's mother.

'You've come on the wrong day.

'Gary Gribble's birthday party is TOMORROW.'

Then Donna-Jane SCREAMED and STAMPED and SHOUTED and ROARED and GRIZZLED and GROUCHED and GRUMBLED and SULKED and WAILED and SOBBED and SIGHED all the way home.

And she tripped up the step and threw down the secret present all wrapped up in shiny paper.

It bumped down the front step ...

... and out rolled ...

An apple! A very big apple.

'Why have you wrapped a very big apple up in shiny paper as a secret present for Gary Gribble?' said Donna-Jane's mother.

'Because I wanted his present for ME,' said Donna-Jane.

'I liked it best. So I swopped.'

'Tomorrow is another day,' said Donna-Jane's mother.

'And a good thing too.

'You have not been a very nice little girl today, Donna-Jane.'

'But I am pretty,' said Donna-Jane. 'So I must be nice.'

Donna-Jane's father looked at Donna-Jane.

He looked at the very big apple.

The apple looked beautiful.

It had a red and shiny skin.

But it was very, very ripe.

It was very, very soft and bruised.

Donna-Jane's father cut the apple open with a knife.

The apple was brown and mushy and bad inside.

'UGH!' said Donna-Jane. 'YUK!'

'That's a horrid apple inside.

'But it looked nice,' said Donna-Jane.

'That's not always too important,' said Donna-Jane's father. 'It's just the same with us.'

'God doesn't mind too much what we look like.

'It's what we're really like that matters.'

Donna-Jane thought hard about that.

She remembered once eating a wizenedy, wrinkled old apple that looked very peculiar.

But it had tasted good.

Next day Donna-Jane started all over again to go to Gary Gribble's birthday party.

This time she wore a jumper and a skirt and welly boots.

And a BIG SMILE for everyone – for Dad and Mum and the cat and nice old Mr Joe and nice chatty Mrs Molly and Gary Gribble's mother and Gary Gribble and HERSELF – in the mirror.

And Donna-Jane gave Gary Gribble his proper secret present, all wrapped up again, in shiny paper.

Gary Gribble grinned and said a big thank you – and Donna-Jane found she almost liked him after all!

'I think I feel nicer inside now,' said Donna-Jane.

'Good,' said Donna-Jane's mother and father together.

'But what ARE you giving Gary Gribble, all wrapped up in shiny paper?'

'It's a … SECRET!' said Donna-Jane.

Dear God, we know that we can look nice, but still be bad or naughty inside. We know, too, that it's what we're really like that matters to you. Please help us to be good and grow more loving. *Amen*

Floppy Poppy and the blue umbrella

It was a very wet and rainy summer day. Robert had to spend the day with his friend, Simon, who he didn't know very well, and Simon's Mum, Pauline, who he didn't really know at all, and Simon's sister, Josie, who was only little, and Kevin's puppy, Rusty, that was very bouncy and barked a great deal.

And Robert didn't want to go. Sometimes, Pauline looked after other children as well, and he wouldn't know them at all. Robert wanted to stay at home and play with his own toys.

'Why can't I stay at home with you?' grumbled Robert. 'And why does it have to be raining? And why can't I go to playschool?'

'Because it's not a playschool day,' said Mum. 'And I've got to work extra at the supermarket. And I didn't make it rain. Now come along and get ready.'

Mum and Robert got out of the car and ran through the wet drops under Mum's blue umbrella to Simon's house. As they walked up the garden path Robert noticed how bedraggled everything looked in the rain. The flower beds were all muddy and damp. There were some red poppies, but they had all flopped over and looked rather sad and fed up.

'They're floppy poppies,' said Robert as Mum pushed him in through the door and said goodbye. That was how he felt, damp and droopy and fed up.

Inside, Simon and Josie and their mum, Pauline, were busy doing all sorts of things at once. There were two other children as well, a boy and a girl that Robert had never seen before, and one or two others who were all making lots of mess, cutting and glueing and zooming toy cars over the carpet. Rusty, the puppy, ran in and out, getting under all the feet and chewing an old slipper.

'This is Jasvir and this is Reena,' said Pauline, showing Robert where the other boy and girl were building a tower of bricks with Simon.

Robert didn't know what to play with. Then Pauline said, 'There's a big box of junk material here, Robert. We can make all sorts of things. You could make something to take home.'

Suddenly, all the children wanted to make something from the junk box. They all rummaged about, pulling out egg boxes and silver paper and yogurt cartons.

'I'm making a car!' said Simon.

'I'm making a house!' said Reena.

'I'm making a crocodile!' said Jasvir, waving an egg-box that looked like crocodile teeth.

'I'm making dinner,' said Josie, holding a paper plate.

Robert found himself holding an empty squeezy bottle in one hand and an old sock in the other, and he didn't know quite what to do with them. He put the squeezy bottle into the sock and wrapped some bright red floppy material round it and looked at it. It looked a bit like a person, especially when he found some glue and stuck some wool on top for hair. This was fun. He worked hard, putting a funny smiley face on the doll with a felt pen. Then he made the doll dance up and down.

'Why, Robert, that's a super doll you've made,' said Pauline, coming over to look. 'It looks like the poppies in my garden.'

Robert remembered the poppies in the rain.

'It's Floppy Poppy,' said Robert.

Everybody liked Robert's doll very much. It sat up to lunch with them, next to Robert. He ate a big plate of sausages and chips and then some ice-cream. He felt happy!

'I love the doll I've made,' said Robert to Jasvir and Reena and Simon and Josie and Pauline. 'You can play with it but you must be very careful because it's mine really.'

They were all so busy playing after lunch that Robert didn't notice that the rain had stopped. The sun came out and the children all ran into the garden to play. The garden dried up quickly in the hot summer sunshine.

Then Pauline came outside. She was carrying Robert's mum's blue umbrella.

'Your mum went off in such a hurry she left it behind,' said Pauline. 'I'll open it up and put it here on the grass in the sun to dry.'

The children all played together in the garden for the rest of the afternoon with Floppy Poppy and the sand-pit and the trikes and the swing. The puppy, Rusty, ran in and out, too. Then they all had a pretend tea party with little biscuits that Josie and Pauline had made. By the end of the afternoon it was so hot that they made the blue umbrella into a sunshade and sat under it for a minute. It made a nice house for Floppy Poppy, too. Then they all raced off again to have turns on the swing.

Suddenly, Robert remembered Floppy Poppy. He looked under the blue umbrella to make sure she was all right – but she wasn't there! She'd disappeared!

'My doll! She's gone!' wailed Robert.

The others all came to look.

'She's run away,' said Reena.

'I know I put her there. She was having her tea,' explained Robert sadly. 'Did one of you take her?'

But nobody had. Pauline came out to help and they hunted all over the garden – in the sandpit, under the trees, beside the swing and in the shed, but there was no sign of Robert's doll. They all went into the house.

'I'll have a look in the kitchen,' said Pauline. 'But just a minute – I can hear Rusty barking somewhere. I think he's run upstairs.'

Pauline went up to look and the children followed.

'Oh you naughty Rusty!' said Pauline.

There was Rusty on the landing, playing with Floppy Poppy! He was pulling at her hair and chewing her.

Robert was upset.

'That's my doll,' he sobbed. 'Naughty, stupid dog, you've taken my doll and spoiled her. It was mine. I made her and I like her a lot.'

'Of course you do,' said Pauline kindly. 'We all love things we've made. I'll help you mend her right away.'

Robert dried his eyes and and everyone crowded round and helped with glue and more material. Soon Floppy Poppy was as good as new, even with a new smiling face, and Robert felt much happier again. He even quite liked the puppy, Rusty, after all, especially when she picked up the slipper again and shook it and brought it to him and made him laugh. After all, she was only a baby dog.

Floppy Poppy was mended just as Mum knocked at the door to collect Robert.

'I've had a lovely day,' said Robert. 'I've made new friends, and I've had sausages and chips and ice-cream and I've played in the sandpit and I've been on the swing and had a tea party and made a doll and I think I want to go to Simon's house again.'

'Robert's doll had an adventure,' said Pauline to Mum. 'We thought she'd run away. We even had to mend her smile.'

'She looks really happy now,' said Robert to Mum. 'I do like my doll. Making things is fun.'

PRAYER

Dear God, who made the world, I like making things, too. I like painting and cutting and sticking and making models. I love the things I've made. I know you love everything that you've made, so I know you love me too. *Amen*

The flowers that disappeared

Danny lived in a big, busy, noisy city. It was always full of people who hurried and bustled everywhere, and buses and cars that made lots of exhaust fumes, and lorries that rumbled and hooted and tooted all day and all night.

Danny lived with his dad in a cosy flat over a florist's shop. The shop sold all sorts of flowers that smelled lovely and looked beautiful when they were all wrapped in crunchy cellophane for customers. Sometimes Danny helped in the shop. A lot of the customers knew him, like Mr Jenkins who often bought flowers for Mrs Jenkins, and old Mrs King who sometimes came in to buy a plant for her window-box.

Danny went to school each day. He liked his school, and he liked his teachers, and he liked his cosy flat and his dad and the flowers and the shop. But sometimes he wished that the town wasn't quite so big and busy and noisy.

Then one hot summer day Dad said,

'We're going to have a holiday, Danny. Next week we're going to stay for a fortnight with Aunty Jean in the country.'

Next week! Danny was excited.

'A fortnight – two whole weeks!' said Danny happily.

They went on holiday in Dad's van, and it was a long journey. Aunty Jean lived in the countryside in a cottage. She painted pictures and made pots that people sometimes came to buy. Her kitchen shelves were covered with jam-jars of wild flowers and grasses, and feathers and fir cones and shells and pebbles and pens and pencils and all sorts of interesting things. The cottage was in a lane near a farm with green fields and sheep and cows and horses. There were chickens who laid real eggs just like the ones you bought in the supermarket in cardboard boxes.

One day, Aunty Jean took Danny out for a walk and a sandwich picnic. They saw sheep and horses and they walked through a field of cows and they looked at wild flowers and listened to the birds singing.

'There are so many trees,' said Danny. 'Everything is all green and quiet. And it smells nice everywhere. God made the country nicely.'

'He did, but he made people in the town nicely, too,' said Aunty Jean.

Then, when they were nearly home, Danny said,

'Look! There's a blue field! It looks like the sea!'

'It's not the sea,' smiled Aunty Jean. 'The sea's quite a long way away.'

They went down a lane and across a field to see the blue field more closely.

'That's a field full of flowers called flax,' said Aunty Jean. 'It can be used to make oil, or sometimes cloth, called linen. The flowers are blue.'

'I like it,' said Danny. 'I want to show Dad later.'

At tea-time Danny said to Dad,

'I saw a blue field today.'

'Really?' laughed Dad. 'Don't you mean a green field?'

'No,' said Danny. 'I mean a blue field. Come on, I'll show you.'

He took Dad's hand and they walked down the lane together while Aunty Jean cleared the tea things. It was beginning to get dusk. But Danny couldn't find the right field.

'I know this is the way we came home,' said Danny, puzzled.

'Perhaps it was a different road,' said Dad. 'The lanes and fields all look alike. Come on, I think we must go home now. There's Aunty Jean come to meet us.'

Aunty Jean joined them.

'Our blue flowers have disappeared,' said Danny sadly.

Aunty Jean laughed.

'I think you'll find they're right here in this field, just where you thought they were,' she said. 'Look more closely, Danny.'

This was very mysterious! Dad and Danny followed Aunty Jean and they went into the green field. It was full of little green flowers, tightly closed. Aunty Jean picked one and showed it to Danny.

'Now look,' said Aunty Jean.

Danny peered hard into the flower.

'Oh!' said Danny in great surprise. 'It's blue inside! It was all shut up!'

He clapped his hands in delight.

'Some flowers close right up at night when it gets cool and dark,' explained Aunty Jean.

'So you did see a blue field after all,' said Dad.

'And a green one!' said Aunty Jean. 'That field was teasing you, Danny.'

After that, Danny looked at the field of flax every day, sometimes in the morning, sometimes in the evening, just to make sure.

'I don't want to go home,' said Danny at the end of their stay. 'I like living in the country. I like all the things that God made, especially the blue-green field with all those lovely flowers.'

'Home's special,' said Aunty Jean. 'Home's a good place. God has made people, too – all your friends and all the people in the buses and trains and in the shop - and wherever you are he's always there, everywhere in the world, and he doesn't change. He's always the same.'

Danny thought about the field that kept changing colour, and he was glad that God was always the same. After his stay in the country Danny sent a picture to Aunty Jean. It was a special picture. On the front it was full of blue flowers, and Danny wrote 'Day' very carefully in his best writing. On the back it was full of green flowers, and it said 'Night'. It took Danny quite a long time, and while he worked at it he thought what a beautiful and interesting world God had made.

Aunty Jean pinned it up in her kitchen above the shelf with the wild flowers and the pebbles and the feathers and fir cones and all the pens and pencils.

'I saw blue flowers that turned green and disappeared,' Danny said to old Mrs King when she came into the shop to buy an African violet.

'Really?' said old Mrs King. 'You make sure my purple African violet doesn't change colour!'

'I saw blue flowers that turned green and disappeared,' Danny said to Mr Jenkins when he came into the shop to buy flowers for Mrs Jenkins.

'Really? said Mr Jenkins. 'You make sure my red

roses don't disappear!'

'I saw blue flowers that turned green,' Danny told his teacher and his friends at school.

'That's interesting, Danny,' said his teacher.

'Yes, it was,' said Danny, and he told his class all about the flowers that disappeared. He thought to himself how wonderful God must be to take such a lot of trouble over all the plants and flowers that he had made.

And people, too.

PRAYER

Thank you God, for the wonderful, interesting world that you have made for us all to enjoy. Thank you for the beauty of the countryside, and for all the people in the town. *Amen*

God's Wonderful World

I live in a wonderful world
Of flowers and birds and trees;
Mountains, hills and rivers,
Butterflies and bees.

I live in a wonderful world
Of coloured rainbow light;
Red and yellow, green and blue,
So beautiful and bright.

I live in a wonderful world
Of creatures big and small
That prowl or walk or run,
Fly or swim or crawl.

I live in a wonderful world
Of ice and frost and snow;
Clouds and rain and fog,
Sunshine's gentle glow.

I live in a wonderful world
Of boats and trains and cars;
Aeroplanes and rockets,
Flying to the stars.

I live in a wonderful world
Of people under the sun;
People young and old –
God loves every one.

I live in a wonderful world
Of wonderful, wonderful things;
Thank you God for each new day
That each new morning brings.

Frazer's friends

It was the end of winter, and Frazer and Matthew had been at school for nearly two terms. One day, Frazer slipped on some ice and fell over on his way to school. It was a nasty fall and Frazer broke one of his arms and twisted his ankle and cut his knee. He had to wear a plaster on his arm, and a bandage round his ankle and his cut knee.

Frazer's best schoolfriend was Matthew. They played a lot together in the playground and in the sandpit and with a football and on the new slide. Matthew loved school, especially football and the new slide. The snow soon melted away into springtime and the children could play outdoors again, but Frazer had to wear the plaster on his arm and hop about for quite a while after that.

'Frazer can't play football with me properly now,' grumbled Matthew to Mum. 'It's boring.'

'That's not very kind,' said Mum. 'I expect it's boring for Frazer.'

Mrs Wilson, and Miss Becky who helped, and the children at school were kind to Frazer. They helped him and they practised writing their names on the plaster on his arm, and drew funny pictures all over it.

'Come and do some painting with Frazer,' said Mrs
Wilson to Matthew. 'He'd like that. Come and help
him hold the paint pots.'

But Matthew wouldn't join in. He turned away and
pretended he was busy writing a story in his news book.

'I'll come instead,' said Reshma. 'I would like to
paint with Frazer.'

'Why don't you make a junk model with Frazer,' suggested Miss Becky later on, to Matthew. 'You could
make a space ship together.'

'I'm doing sums,' said Matthew.

'I'll come,' said Tom. 'I'd love to make a space ship.'

'Frazer can't run or walk properly,' complained
Matthew to Dad. 'He won't be able to play with me for
ages. He still has to have a silly old plaster on his arm
and he can't run about properly and play football.'

'It's not silly,' said Dad. 'You're the one who's being
silly, and not very kind. The plaster and the bandage
are helping Frazer to get better as fast as he can.'

One day, Frazer brought a new jigsaw puzzle to
school. He'd been given it as a present to help him get
well soon. One by one the other children crowded
round to play with the jigsaw.

Matthew felt very left out. Frazer was *his* best friend.
It wasn't fair. Nobody was playing with *him*.

Then Matthew did something very naughty. When
the children were having their drink and he thought
nobody was looking, he muddled up the jigsaw that
had been put to one side on a different table. Then he
hid some of the pieces in his pocket. He ran outside
very quickly at playtime to be first on that new slide –
and tripped over. He fell very hard on the ground.

'I've hurt my hand and my knees,' sobbed Matthew

abc

miserably to Mrs Wilson and Miss Becky as they picked him up. 'They're all grazed and achy and sore.'

He wanted his mum and dad. He wanted someone to be kind to him.

Matthew cried and sniffed and fished in his pocket for his hanky.

And out fell the pieces of jigsaw!

'Oh, Matthew,' said Mrs Wilson. 'How did they get there?'

'Oh dear,' said Miss Becky, and the children all crowded round to stare at Matthew.

'That's my jigsaw!' said Frazer indignantly.

'That was very naughty, wasn't it?' said Mrs Wilson sternly as she washed his knees.

'You must give the pieces back to Frazer straight away and say sorry,' said Miss Becky.

Matthew began to feel sorry and unhappy. The other children didn't want to play with him because he'd been unkind. He thought,

'Perhaps it would be more fun to play together again. Perhaps I've not been very kind.'

Matthew helped Frazer finish the jigsaw. It was a picture of two smiling cats.

'I've missed you being my best friend,' said Frazer.

'So have I,' said Matthew, and he drew the funniest face of all on Frazer's plaster.

Please God, help us to be kind to each other and to help each other, especially people who are hurt or ill or lonely or sad. *Amen*

The invisible mighty monster

Monkey swung in the trees.

'OOOOOOOOO!' blew a loud and blustery voice like an invisible mighty monster monkey. 'Watch out, Monkey, here I come!'

Monkey heard the mighty monster monkey coming and she ran and climbed and hid in the leaves.

'OOOOOOOOO!' blew the monster again, huffing and puffing. 'I can see YOOOOOOOOOU!'

Monkey felt the mighty monster monkey touch her fur. The monster was big and scary!

Monkey thought she was safe, quite safe, because she was quick and clever and could outmonkey any old monster. She ran from branch to branch, knocking down leaves and twigs and fruits. But the monster saw Monkey and BLEW her nearly off the face of the earth. Then it went clattering away.

But not before a coconut had landed on Monkey's head!

Snake slithered along the ground.

'OOOOOOOOO!' blew a loud and blustery voice like an invisible scary monster snake. 'Watch out, Snake, here I come!'

Snake heard the scary monster snake coming and he wiggled and wriggled along the ground.

'OOOOOOOOO!' blew the monster again, snuffling and sniffling. 'I can see YOOOOOOOOOU!'

Snake felt the warm breath of the scary monster snake on his skin. The monster was big and scary!

Snake thought he was safe, quite safe, because he was smart and slithery and could outsnake any old monster. He wriggled and slithered across the hot, sunny path. But the monster saw Snake and BLEW him nearly off the face of the earth. Then it went rustling away.

But not before the monster had blown dust all over Snake!

Butterfly fluttered in and out of the flowers.

'OOOOOOOOO!' blew a loud and blustery voice like an invisible big and bothersome monster butterfly. 'Watch out, Butterfly, here I come!'

Butterfly heard the big and bothersome monster butterfly coming and she fluttered about in the flowers.

'OOOOOOOOO!' blew the monster again, whiffling and whistling. 'I can see YOOOOOOOOOU!'

Butterfly felt her wings shiver and tremble as the monster came closer. It blew her about. The monster was big and scary!

Butterfly thought she was safe, quite safe, because she was dainty and pretty and could outbutterfly any old monster. She flitted and fluttered in and out of the flowers. But the monster saw Butterfly and BLEW her nearly off the face of the earth. Then it went skimming away.

But not before Butterfly felt dizzy and her wings were crumpled!

Parrot flew about in the trees.

'OOOOOOOOO!' blew a loud and blustery voice like an invisible petrifying monster parrot. 'Watch out, Parrot, here I come!'

Parrot heard the petrifying monster parrot coming and he flew very fast and squawked very loudly in the leaves.

'OOOOOOOOO!' blew the monster again, screeching and howling. 'I can see YOOOOOOOOOU!'

Parrot felt as if his bright-coloured feathers were turning pale as the monster came towards him. The monster was big and scary!!

Parrot thought he was safe, quite safe, because he was bright and beautiful and colourful and had a big curved beak and could outparrot any old monster. And he could talk! He said:

'I can see YOOOOOOOOU, TOOOOOO!'

But the monster saw and heard Parrot and BLEW him nearly off the face of the earth. Then it went screeching away.

But not before Parrot's feathers were very, very ruffled!

Small Tiger sat in the long grass.

'OOOOOOOOO!' blew a loud and blustery voice like an invisible, terrifying monster tiger. 'Watch out, Tiger, here I come!'

Small Tiger heard the terrifying monster tiger coming and he didn't run or slither or fly or squawk or any of those things at all. He didn't even growl. He just SAT STILL.

And because Small Tiger sat still and quiet and didn't move, and because his stripes were nearly the same colour as the dry grass and the dappled leaves moving in the sunlight, he couldn't be seen or heard. He looked like the grass. He was almost invisible, too!

And the blowy, scary, invisible, terrifying, petrifying, whiffling, whistling, bothersome, loud and blustery mighty monster just laughed and laughed and laughed.

And vanished right away!

PRAYER

We praise you, God, for all the different animals that you have made, and especially for their wonderful patterns. Help us not to forget that it is you who has made the animals so carefully, with all their stripes and spots and colours that hide them or keep them safe. *Amen*

(Who do you think the monster was?)

Katie in the kitchen

Katie's mum was busy cooking in the kitchen. She was cooking little biscuits and tarts and cakes, and a birthday rainbow cake made of dollops of different coloured sponge. It was Katie's fifth birthday the next day, and all her friends were coming to tea.

The kitchen smelt good. Dad and Katie came into the kitchen.

'Can I help?' said Katie. 'My dolls and teddies are tired of playing with me today. I like cooking, and I'm quite grown up now because I'm nearly five.'

'You're quite an old lady,' teased Dad. 'Mmm ... the kitchen smells nice. Can I help too?'

'I think one helper will be quite enough,' said Mum firmly, and Dad laughed and went outdoors to cut the grass ready for Katie's party the next day.

Katie climbed on a chair so that she could reach the worktop, and wore her own plastic apron. Mum gave her a bowl and spoon, and Katie found her own toy rolling pin and biscuit cutters.

'I'm ready to start cooking,' said Katie, waving her wooden spoon and picking up a big bag of flour.

Cooking was fun. All the things like sugar and eggs

and flour made such lovely things to eat.

Katie rolled out some pastry.

She cut out biscuits into pretty stars and circles.

She put jam into some tarts.

She decorated with cherries and she sprinkled hundreds and thousands and she cut out tops for some little cakes to look like butterfly wings.

Mum put Katie's cooking on to a tray.

'Oh dear,' said Katie, looking at it all. The pastry looked rather grey, and the biscuits were slightly lopsided, and the jam tarts had oozed jam over their edges. There seemed to be sticky cherries and hundreds and thousands and flour all over the kitchen.

'The butterfly cakes don't look much like butterflies,' said Katie sadly.

'Never mind,' said Mum. 'They'll taste nice. Now let's ice your birthday cake.'

Mum wrote 'Katie' in icing on top of the rainbow birthday cake.

'Can I put a '5' on as well?' said Katie, reaching for the icing nozzle, while Mum went to take some sausage rolls out of the oven.

It was quite difficult writing a squiggly '5' in icing, so Katie tried again ... and again.

'It's very wobbly,' said Katie.

'Oh dear,' said Mum, looking at Katie's handiwork. Then she said,

'Katie – you've written 555! You really ARE grown up!'

'You are a VERY old lady,' laughed Dad, when he saw Katie's birthday cake. 'Five hundred and fifty-five!'

'I don't think my friends will like my cooking much,' said Katie. 'But I know now what to play with my dolls

and teddies. They can have a tea-party. They're quite hungry now, and they'll like eating all the things I cooked for them.'

And they did – but Katie and Dad had to help them eat it all up!

Learning to cook is fun. Thank you, God, for cosy kitchens, nice smells and warm cookers. Thank you for busy worktops and splashy sinks. Thank you for cupboards and fridges. Thank you for butter and sugar and flour and eggs, and for mums and dads who help me learn how to cook. *Amen*

Yum Yum Yum (finger rhyme)

1 crusty loaf to share with Dad and Mum;

2 fish fingers, yum yum yum.

3 orange oranges, juicy and sweet;

4 red cherries, a lunch-box treat.

5 ripe bananas in a bunch, and THEN ...

6 brown eggs from a big, brown hen.

7 round tomatoes,

8 green peas;

9 jars of honey from the busy, buzzy bees.

10 rosy apples growing on a tree;

All God's gifts for you and me!
(clap hands on last line)

Kevin and the clonker

It was autumn. Kevin had a conker, and he was very proud of it. It was a big, brown, shiny conker that he had found under a horse chestnut tree on his way to school, as he and Mum walked along near the edge of the common. The conker was threaded on a string.

'My conker's a really good one,' boasted Kevin to his friends, swinging it about on its string. 'It's a big one. It's really hard, look – CLONK! It makes a good noise. It's not just a conker – it's a clonker!'

Kevin carried the conker everywhere in his pocket on its piece of string. He clonked all his friends' conkers in the playground and he clonked at the door when he came home from school and he clonked at the window.

'You be careful with that clonker,' said Mum. 'You'll clonk something that isn't meant to be clonked, like my best cups and saucers or that window. You'll break the glass.'

Kevin stopped clonking the window and looked through it instead. A grey squirrel ran across the garden with something in its mouth.

'It's carrying a nut!' said Kevin. 'But it's not a clonker. It's too small.'

'We haven't any conker trees in our garden,' said Mum. 'I expect the squirrel has found a little chestnut or a beech nut or an acorn. He might be going to bury it and hide it.'

'Why?' asked Kevin.

'They bury nuts to store away for the winter,' said Mum. 'But often they forget where they've hidden them and then they can't find them again when they're hungry.'

Kevin was glad that Mum didn't forget where she'd put the baked beans and bread and eggs in the kitchen.

On the way to school next day Kevin watched another squirrel. It ran around under the trees.

'That one's got something in its mouth, too!' said Kevin. 'And look – it's hiding it!'

The squirrel had an acorn in its paws. Kevin and Mum watched as the squirrel dug furiously in the ground, pushed the acorn into the hole, then patted it down. Then it scampered away.

Kevin tried to chase the squirrel, swinging his conker. The conker caught the face of his friend, Nadim, who was on his way to school, too.

'Ouch!' said Nadim. 'That hurt!'

He grabbed at Kevin's conker. It came off its string as Kevin grabbed it back again.

'My clonker's spoiled,' said Kevin angrily. 'It's all knocked about.'

'That's because you've been clonking at everything so much,' said Mum. 'Now say sorry to Nadim and hurry along or you'll be late for school.'

Kevin hid the clonker right away in his pocket. On the way home from school he showed Mum a little pot with some earth in it.

'It's a flower bulb,' said Kevin. 'Our teacher helped

us plant them and we've got to put them in the dark and forget about them and then they'll make flowers in the spring. Can I plant my clonker too, like the squirrel, here on the common? Then I'll dig it up in the spring and have it to clonk with again.'

So Kevin and Mum poked the clonker in some earth under a tree with a knobbly branch.

'I'll remember exactly where,' said Kevin. He wondered if the squirrel was watching him.

Then it was the winter-time, and Kevin really did forget all about the bulb, and the conker too, because lots of exciting things happened like Christmas and parties and holidays and snow.

One spring day it was Kevin's teacher's birthday. Kevin bought her a little bag of sweets for a present. He carried it to school carefully, walking along with Mum by the edge of the common as usual.

Kevin noticed a squirrel up a tree, and he remembered his conker. He'd forgotten all about it – just like the squirrel! The squirrel ran down the tree trunk, and before Mum could stop him Kevin chased after it.

'My conker's here somewhere,' said Kevin. 'Just here, I'm sure, where it's all muddy; yes, right here, because there's that knobbly branch.'

Then ... Kevin tripped over a tree root and fell headlong, twisting his foot and banging his head very hard on the ground.

The sweets flew out of the bag and into the mud. They were spoiled. Kevin sat very still for a moment. Then he cried and cried because he'd grazed his knee and it was bleeding and his head ached a lot and his leg hurt. He couldn't see where he'd planted the conker, anyway. Where he'd fallen was all twigs and leaves and buds and green shoots poking out of the ground.

Kevin had to stay at home from school for a week. One day when he was beginning to feel better, he looked in one of the cupboards where his old toys were kept, for something different to play with. The cupboard was rather dark. As Kevin rummaged about he felt some earth ...

'My bulb!' said Kevin to Mum. 'Look!'

There were leaves just showing above the earth. But they were very pale.

'Has it died?' said Kevin.

'No,' said Mum. 'But it would like some sunshine and light and a drink of water and fresh air.'

Then Kevin said,

'I know – I can take my bulb to my teacher for a happy birthday present when it's got flowers!'

'She'll like that,' smiled Mum.

Kevin's teacher did like the bulb. It had turned into a beautiful blue hyacinth with a wonderful smell.

Kevin looked and looked again on the common for the hole where he'd planted the conker.

'I shall never find it again,' said Kevin sadly. 'I know it was near here, because of the knobbly branch. But it's hard to see because of the grass and things growing up.'

Mum didn't answer. She was pointing at a new green shoot coming up. The shoot had a few tiny leaves. Suddenly Kevin remembered how the bulb he'd planted had turned into a beautiful hyacinth after it had rested in the darkness.

'That's my clonker!' said Kevin. 'It's growing into a tree. It's a baby clonker tree!'

Kevin didn't mind a bit that he wouldn't be able to play with the conker. It would be much more exciting to watch it turn into a tree that would grow bigger and bigger until it reached the sky. And besides, there'd be lots more brown, shiny, clonky conkers again, next autumn.

Conkers and squirrels are fun! Thank you Go, for the seasons that change into spring and summer and autumn and winter. It's wonderful how the nuts and plants and bulbs live and die and rest and grow again. *Amen*

Lucy at the library

Lucy was learning to read, and it was difficult.

'I'm trying hard,' sighed Lucy to Mum, as they walked to the library with their dog, Sally, one day. 'I can read my name because it's on my mug and my plate, and it's on my toy bag, and I can read Sally's name because it's on her collar. But there are so many letters and squiggles to learn, and I forget what they all mean.'

'You'll learn one day soon,' said Mum. 'You're very nearly reading. And today I'm going to arrange for you to join the library, Lucy. Then you'll be able to choose your own books to borrow and take home.'

'I think I'd rather play with my dolls and ride my trike and go on the swings than read,' said Lucy. 'It's easier and much more fun. But it'll be nice to borrow some books, especially if they've got pictures.'

Mum tied Sally up outside the library, which was busy and crowded. It was full of people as well as books.

'Just wait a minute,' said Mum. 'I'll choose my books quickly, then we'll go into the children's library and find some books for you.'

Mum seemed to take ages choosing books, and Lucy soon got tired. She couldn't stay near Mum anyway because of all the other grown-ups in the way. So while Mum was looking at a book, Lucy pushed past them and went into the part of the library that was especially for children.

This part of the library was empty. The bigger children were at school and there weren't any little ones there today. Lucy began to look at the books on the lower shelves. There were other books in wooden boxes where you could sit down and see them easily.

There were so many! The covers were bright and cheerful with such a lot of different pictures, animals and children and houses and colours and patterns.

There were more books, too, piled quite high on a table, waiting to be tidied away on to the shelves. There was a big one on the top that appeared to have a bright cover. Lucy could just see the back and the edges sticking out, and they were red. As nobody was looking, she climbed on to the table and knelt up to see the book.

The picture on the cover was of the outside of a house with steps leading up to the front door. It looked rather like a dolls' house. There were windows. One of the windows had a boy and a girl peeping out with a cat. There were some squiggly words over the house that Lucy didn't understand, except,

'My name!' said Lucy. 'Well I can read that. A book for me!'

She thought how nice it would be to be able to read all the words. Then something very exciting happened – just as she was about to turn the cover to the first page, she found she wasn't in the library any more – she was standing on the front step of the house. Somehow she was turning the page ... and walking right in!

'Oh!' cried Lucy. 'This is an adventure!'

The dolls' house seemed to be arranged rather like Lucy's own doll's house. There were beds and chairs and tables and cups and saucers and cooking pots. There were people sitting on the chairs. Lucy ran in delight from room to room looking at everything carefully. Then she realised that everything had its name beside it, just like her own name on her mug and plate and toy bag at home. She looked carefully at its name label.

'Meeow!' said a little voice, and there was a small black and white cat beside Lucy. 'I'm going to help you read. Let's start with me. I'm a – '

'Cat!' said Lucy, looking at a name on its collar. She was too surprised to say that reading was hard.

'There you are!' said the cat. 'You see, it's not so difficult is it? Only twenty-six letters to learn. You've just read a word! Meeow! Come on – follow me! Do what I do and say what I say. I'm the copy-cat!'

This was great fun. Lucy followed the copy-cat all over the house calling out the names of chairs and tables and cups and plates and beds.

'I can do it!' said Lucy. 'That's a ... window! and a ...'

'Door!' helped the copy-cat.

'Yes, door, door, door!' shouted Lucy happily and so loudly that all the little dolls' house people turned and looked at her. Two of the doll children, a boy and a girl, ran up and took her by each hand, and they all went through the back door of the house into a garden with flowers and apple trees and butterflies. Again, there were neat names on everything.

'Oh, it's so beautiful!' said Lucy, smelling the flowers. Lucy and the boy and girl ran over the green grass and the copy-cat helped again.

'Boy Girl!' said Lucy, as the boy and girl ran ahead, turning to wave goodbye. 'Tree! Flower! Grass! Hedge!'

At one corner of the garden was a small gate. Lucy thought that was where the boy and girl had vanished, but she wasn't too sure ... Beyond the garden Lucy could see more trees, then houses and streets and buses and cars. Then there was countryside and mountains in the far distance, and sea and other countries. There were lots of people. Then sky that seemed to go on for ever into space where there was a sun and a moon and stars ... They all had their names written on, too, in silver and gold and all the beautiful colours of the rainbow. This was an exciting and wonderful world!!

'Off you go now,' said the copy-cat, giving Lucy a gentle nudge towards the gate.

Then: 'WOOF!' barked a dog's voice from somewhere nearby, and the copy-cat said, 'MEEOOO-OOoooooow ...' and vanished.

Lucy went through the gate, after reading its name and saying 'Gate!' as she did so. It swung behind her and Lucy tumbled half-way down the step on the other side.

'Oh!' cried Lucy. 'Why, I'm back on the front step of the dolls' house – and it's got a name, too, oh, what does it say? I need the copy-cat to help me.'

She looked back at the house, and suddenly the squiggly letters began to make sense.

'Lucy ... Lucy's ... house!' read Lucy. 'That's right! That's my name – and that's a house!'

She thought she saw the copy-cat inside the house now at one of the windows, but she wasn't too sure. Then Lucy slithered down the last step and the house started to fade away ... and Lucy found she was falling off the table, just where she had been, looking at the house on the cover of the book. Nothing had changed, except for one thing – Lucy had started to learn to read!

'Lucy's House,' Lucy read out loud.

'Woof!' said Sally, who had broken loose from her lead and burst into the library.

'Lucy!' said Mum, coming in to find her. 'Lucy! You're reading!'

'Yes,' said Lucy. 'I've been in a dolls' house, you see, and a copy-cat helped me to say all the names and I went in a garden and there were apple trees and mountains and people and I said their names and – '

'Lucy!' laughed Mum. 'I think you've been dreaming! You're telling me stories! And I've only been away a few seconds.'

'I haven't been dreaming,' said Lucy indignantly. 'I've been very awake. But I shall be able to tell you stories soon, because I'm learning to read. You said I'd learn to read if I went to the library, and now I can. Can I take home lots of books please, and this one especially?'

Lucy did. And although she turned the pages of the book called 'Lucy's House', and looked and looked, she never found the boy, or the girl or the little cat again. But Lucy knew that even when she was an old, old lady, and had read all the books in the world, she would always remember the day she learned to read.

PRAYER

Thank you, God, for the wonderful world of letters and words and books. Help me to read so that I can enjoy stories, and learn about many interesting things. *Amen*

The very unhelpful princess

Once upon a time, in the country of Ever-Ever Land, lived Princess Petunia. She lived in a palace in the town of Hoopla where there were all sorts of other people – her father and mother, the King and Queen, and children and teachers and milkmen and shopkeepers and restaurant owners and farmers and chimney sweeps and petrol-pump attendants and window cleaners – and Mr Postman, who collected all the letters and posted them every day. The pillar-box was on the other side of town from the palace but it had 'Royal Mail' written on it in smart red and gold letters.

One day, Mr Postman collected all the letters as usual from the pillar-box and struggled with his jangly bunch of keys and the pillar-box door and a rather large parcel. Just then, Princess Petunia came running and running all the way from the palace with a very big bundle of letters in one hand and a basket in the other.

'Here you are, Mr Postman,' said Princess Petunia very bossily. 'Take my letters at once. I've written to all my friends to ask if they've found my beautiful, bright and bouncy ball that has bounced right out of the palace garden. Now I must do an errand for the King and Queen and my pet mouse, Squeaky, who need me to buy breakfast.'

She pushed all the letters into the slit of the pillar-box just as Mr Postman had his hand in the slit. And somehow a gust of wind slammed the door shut and Mr Postman's hand jammed in the slit of the pillar-box with all Princess Petunia's letters and the jangly bunch of keys and the rather large parcel.

'I'm STUCK!' said Mr Postman, which he was.

'Oh dear,' said Princess Petunia in some alarm.

'HELP!' said Mr Postman in a very loud voice. 'Get me OUT, little girl. You have been VERY unhelpful.'

Princess Petunia had never been to school and had never learned how to get postmen unstuck from pillar-boxes. And she didn't really want to help anyway, because she wanted to go home and play. So she ran to tell the King and Queen. On the way, she met Mr Milkman on his milk float, so she bought a bottle of milk for the Queen's breakfast, and said,

'Mr Postman has his hand stuck in the pillar-box, and I'm going home to tell the King and Queen because I'm far too little to help.'

'Then I must go and pull him out,' said Mr Milkman, and ran to help Mr Postman. He pulled and pushed – but Mr Postman was well and truly stuck!

Princess Petunia ran on home. On the way she stopped at Mr Butcher's shop and bought a string of sausages for the King's breakfast, and said,

'Mr Postman has his hand stuck in the pillar-box, and I'm going home to tell the King and Queen because I'm far too little AND far too busy to help.'

'Then I must go and pull him out,' said Mr Butcher, and ran to help Mr Postman. He pulled and pushed – but Mr Postman was well and truly stuck!

Princess Petunia ran on home. On the way, she bought a loaf of bread from Mr Baker's shop for both the King and Queen's breakfast, and said,

'Mr Postman has his hand stuck in the pillar-box, and I'm going home to tell the King and Queen because I'm far too little AND far too busy AND far too important to help.'

'Then I must go and pull him out,' said Mr Baker, and ran to help Mr Postman. He pulled and pushed – but Mr Postman was well and truly stuck!

Princess Petunia ran on home. On the way, she bought a bag of humbugs from Mrs Lolly at the sweet shop for her own breakfast, and said,

'Mr Postman has his hand stuck in the pillar-box, and I'm going home to tell the King and Queen because I'm far too little AND far too busy AND far too important AND far too hungry to help.'

'Then I must go and pull him out,' said Mrs Lolly, and ran to help Mr Postman. She pulled and pushed – but Mr Postman was well and truly stuck!

Princess Petunia ran on home. On the way, she met Mr Glass, the window cleaner, polishing the windows of the school next to Signor Spaghetti's restaurant, so she waved her arms and shouted:

'Mr Postman has his hand stuck in the pillar-box, and I'm going home to tell the King and Queen, because I'm far too little AND far too busy AND far too important AND far too hungry AND far too thirsty to help.'

And THEN – all the children in the school looked up from their desks and they saw and heard Princess Petunia, and Signor Spaghetti and all the people in his restaurant next door. And EVERYONE shouted 'HELP!' and they ALL got up and ran to help

Mr Postman.

By now, the whole town knew that Mr Postman had his hand stuck in the pillar-box. They all made a very long, long, long, long, line – even the animals from the farm and all the cats and all the dogs – and they all pushed and pulled. But still Mr Postman was well and truly stuck!

Princess Petunia reached home. She kept the humbugs hidden in her pocket, and she said to the King and the Queen,

'Here are milk and sausages and bread for your breakfast. But you must help Mr Postman. He has his hand stuck in the pillar-box and I'm far too little AND far too busy AND far too important AND far too hungry AND far too thirsty AND far too tired to help.'

By now, Princess Petunia really was feeling rather hungry and thirsty and tired but she did want to go and play, and she did want to eat her humbugs. So she went into the garden to see if her ball had bounced back.

It hadn't. But the palace gardener was there, and he was an elderly and wise gardener. He whispered something very softly to Squeaky Mouse, who was hoping for some breakfast crumbs. Then he said to Princess Petunia,

'You are NOT far too little or far too busy or far too important or far too hungry or far too thirsty or even far too tired to help.'

'What am I then?' said Princess Petunia rather grandly, wondering what he was going to say.

'You are far too PROUD AND SELFISH AND LAZY AND UNHELP – '

'STOP!' said Princess Petunia, putting her hands over her ears.

'No one is too little or too busy or too anything to

help,' went on the gardener. 'Not even you – or even Squeaky Mouse. Sometimes the littlest help can become a big help. Now – let's go at once to see what we can do.'

'Oh ALL RIGHT,' said Princess Petunia, very grouchily and grumpily INDEED. But she was thinking:

'What if the gardener is right? Maybe I am all those horrid things. I will go and help, after all.'

First of all, she strengthened herself by eating six humbugs.

By now, the line of people was very, very, very, VERY long. Everyone was pushing and pulling. But Mr Postman was STILL well and truly stuck!

Everyone bowed and curtsied to the King and the Queen and Princess Petunia as they walked to the end of the line. As they passed Signor Spaghetti he bowed – and Squeaky Mouse ran on to his shoulder and sat on his head and SQUEAKED in his ear – 'EEK!' – and Signor Spaghetti nearly jumped out of his skin!

Now Signor Spaghetti never went anywhere without a giant pepper pot, in case someone needed pepper on their pizza. He had it in his hand now. He jumped so hard and so high in fright that clouds and clouds of pepper flew everywhere, and everybody sneezed – VERY, VERY HARD. They all sneezed so hard that THE DOOR OF THE PILLAR-BOX BLEW OPEN!

Everybody crowded round and helped to get Mr Postman and his hand and his keys and the letters and the parcel out of the slit of the pillar-box.

'Phew,' said Mr Postman. 'That was quite a shamozzle and a scrimmage, I must say.'

'What a commotion,' said the Mayor, bustling up in his gold chain. 'Who caused this disturbance, may I ask?'

'It was ME,' said Princess Petunia, looking down shyly and stroking Squeaky Mouse. 'Well ... sort of.'

'Very good, very good,' boomed the Mayor. 'Excellent. Well done.'

After that, everything became quite simple. Princess Petunia's letters flew about everywhere, and the King's crown fell off, and the Queen's hair became rather untidy, and the dogs chased the cats, and the cats chased Squeaky Mouse all the way back to the Palace. But, otherwise, the town went back to normal. Mr Postman had a cup of tea and a pizza with Signor Spaghetti, and wrapped his hand in a large sling bandage to show how brave he'd been.

The next day there was a knock at the Palace door. It was Mr Postman, and he was carrying the very same parcel that had been wedged in the pillar-box.

'It's for you, Princess Petunia,' said Mr Postman, handing it to her. Inside was the big and bright and bouncing coloured ball!

'But who found it and sent it back to me?' said Princess Petunia.

'It was the gardener – and me,' said Mr Postman. 'When it bounced over the Palace wall AGAIN, the gardener was so tired of going to get it he asked me to keep it for a few days to teach you a lesson. Then I got stuck – thanks to you – and unstuck again, thanks to everyone, even you and little Squeaky Mouse. Let's have a party!'

The whole town of Hoopla went to the party, at Signor Spaghetti's restaurant. The King and Queen and Princess Petunia were invited, and so was Squeaky Mouse, who ate up all the crumbs from all the pizzas.

PRAYER

Help me, God, to do whatever I can to help others, even if it doesn't seem very much. Please use my hands and feet to be as useful as possible. *Amen*

New shoes

It was New Shoes Day. Cheryl needed new shoes and so did her younger brother, David. And so did Mum, and so did Dad. The only member of the family who didn't need new shoes was baby Sean, because he was only tiny, and he only wore bare feet or socks, or bootees when the weather was cold, like now on a winter afternoon.

'Hurry up,' called Mum. 'Dad and I have been ready for ages. The shop will be shut before we get there.'

But Cheryl and David were hunting for Tibby, their tabby cat. Tibby had come to them as a stray not long ago. Mum and Dad couldn't find who her owner was and so Tibby had stayed with them ever since. She was a big, fat, cosy, lazy cat who liked to curl up and go to sleep in the comfiest places she could find.

'We can't find her anywhere,' said Cheryl. 'We've looked all over the house and she's not there. She's vanished!'

'I looked under my bed,' said David. 'I've looked in all the rooms, even the bathroom!'

'See if she's in the cupboard under the stairs where the ironing board and the vacuum cleaner live,' suggested Mum.

But Tibby wasn't there.

'Look behind the curtains, on the window ledges,' suggested Dad.

But Tibby wasn't there, either.

'I think she's run away,' said Cheryl, looking anxious. 'Perhaps she's gone back to where she came from.'

'She might have been chased by a fox or a dog,' said David. 'I wish she'd come home.'

'So do I,' said Cheryl. She loved their tabby cat. Then she remembered that you could ask God to help you. So she whispered to God,

'Please look after Tibby and keep her safe and please bring her home again.'

'Come ON,' said Dad. 'It'll be dark soon. We're never going to buy those shoes. We'll look for Tibby when we get home again.'

So off they all went down the hill into town to the shoe shop in the High Street. Mum pushed baby Sean in the pram. He was well wrapped in his hat and his mittens and his bootees and blankets.

'You'll need shoes soon,' said Mum to Sean. 'You're growing so fast. You're getting bigger and heavier every day.'

The shoe shop was busy and crowded. Mum lifted Sean out and left the pram parked outside the shop.

Choosing shoes took a long time!

Cheryl liked the blue ones but the red ones fitted best.

David said slip-ons but Mum said lace-ups.

Mum wanted shiny, black shoes with low heels but there were only dull, black shoes with high heels.

Dad wanted new slippers but there weren't any the right size.

Baby Sean got bored and wriggled and grizzled and wriggled and squirmed and yelled, and Mum looked anxious and the assistant grew more and more harassed and Dad began to feel annoyed. But at last they left the shop with all their parcels of new shoes, and Mum put baby Sean back in the pram with some of the shopping on top.

Cheryl suddenly remembered Tibby.

'We must hurry home,' said Cheryl to Mum and Dad. 'Then we can look for Tibby again.'

'She might have run away for ever,' said David.

'She might be waiting for us on the step,' said Dad.

'I can't hurry any faster,' said Mum.

'It's hard work getting Sean up the hill,' said Dad, pushing the pram. 'Mum's right, he's getting bigger and heavier every day.'

When they reached home Sean had fallen asleep so Mum left him in the pram in the hall while she laid the table for tea. But there was still no sign of Tibby anywhere. Cheryl and David were so upset they didn't want much tea, and they weren't very interested in their new shoes.

'I know she's run away,' wept Cheryl. 'She's gone back to her other home and we don't know where she is and we'll never see her again.'

'I expect a fox or a dog did chase her away like I said,' said David sadly.

'Well, I want some tea even if you don't,' said Dad. 'I'm hungry after all that hard work. After tea we'll look again.'

'I'm sure she's somewhere safe,' said Mum. 'But baby Sean wants his tea, too, and then we'll all have a big search for Tibby.'

Baby Sean did want his tea. He began to wriggle and whimper and stretch and yawn and kick off his

blankets. Mum went into the hall.

Then – 'Look!' called Mum. 'Cheryl, David, come here! Quickly!'

Cheryl and David ran to look – and there at the end of the pram by Sean's feet was ...

Tibby!

'Tibby!' said Cheryl. 'THAT'S where you were hiding!'

'Tibby!' said David. 'You've been to the shoe shop!'

'She didn't need shoes,' said Dad. 'I think she just wanted a ride. I've never heard of a cat going shoe-shopping!'

'I think she liked Sean's warm blankets, and his warm feet in those bootees,' said Mum.

'She must have climbed in the pram when nobody saw,' said Cheryl, cuddling Tibby and stroking her. Then she had an awful thought. Tibby might have jumped out of the pram in the middle of the busy High Street. She would have been frightened and she wouldn't have known how to get home ... Then Cheryl suddenly remembered that she'd asked God to find Tibby, and to keep Tibby safe.

And he had!

'Thank you, God,' whispered Cheryl. She thought God must like Tibby a lot, too, because God was a wonderful God, and Tibby was a wonderful cat.

Everyone made a big fuss of Tibby. Dad gave her a special tea with some extra fish and milk.

The next day, Mum told Mrs Williams, the next-door-neighbour all about Tibby's adventure, and Mrs Williams said,

'Fancy that!' and told her friend Mrs Brown round the corner who said,

'Fancy that!' and told her sister Mrs Jones in the next road who said,

'Fancy that!' and told her cousin Grace a few streets away all about the tabby cat who went to town. And cousin Grace said,

'Fancy that! That's funny! Old Mr Rogers in a village near here lost his tabby cat. She strayed away and he couldn't find her. He was sad but he's moved right away now and got himself a big dog for company. Funny thing was, he said he knew God would look after her and asked God to find a good home for her.'

'So Tibby's ours for keeps!' said David, cuddling her and listening to her purring loudly.

'You're really ours now,' said Cheryl, nuzzling up close to Tibby's warm, whiskery head. She felt so happy she thought she might purr, too!

'Thank you, God,' whispered Cheryl to God again.

PRAYER

We love our animals and pets, God, all our cats and dogs and budgies and rabbits and tortoises. Help us to look after them and keep them safe. Remind us that we must always remember to feed them properly and give them enough to drink. *Amen*

Cat and Mouse

Squeak! said the mouse.
I like your house.
But if I see the cat - that's THAT!

(This rhyme could be played as a group game based on 'Grandmother's Footsteps', and could be used as a starting point for discussion about animals or pets. The leader, or the leader and children, together say the rhyme very quietly, while the 'mice' creep up to the 'cat'. On the word 'THAT!' (said loudly with a hand clap) the 'cat' turns to see how many 'mice' it can chase and touch.)

Camilla's Christmas stocking

Camilla went Christmas shopping with Mum, and she grumbled nearly all the way. She grumbled because they had to go by bus because the car was being mended, and she grumbled because the shops were hot, and she grumbled because she had to walk a lot. She grumbled because there was a lot to carry, and she grumbled because her favourite long, red socks felt hot and tickly and, well, because she felt grumbly.

'I want a drink,' said Camilla. 'I'm tired.'

'Later,' said Mum. 'But just one more shop first, the big store. I want to buy a scarf for Aunty Debby and a book for Grandpa and some soap for Grandma and some socks for Dad and a tie for Uncle Gerald to give to them on Christmas Day.'

At last, they stopped shopping and sat down in a café. Camilla sighed and scowled and grumbled again because there weren't many currants in her scone and her drink was too fizzy and made her nose feel prickly.

'Oh, Camilla,' said her mum. 'You are being grouchy and grumbly and tiresome today. Whatever is wrong?'

Camilla pouted and muttered something and blew loud prickly bubbles into her drink which didn't please

Mum at all.

At last, they went home again on the bus, laden with shopping.

'I'm tired of Christmas shopping,' said Camilla.

'Already?' said Mum.

'Already,' said Camilla firmly.

When they reached home Camilla was still grumbling, this time because her feet ached from walking round the shops. She went up to her bedroom and took off her shoes and found there was a large hole in one of her favourite long, red socks, so she shoved it crossly into the waste-paper basket. The other one was all right, so Camilla put it under her pillow with the rosebud-patterned pillowcase. It would do nicely for Father Christmas when he came on Christmas morning. The sock was nice and stretchy and would take lots of presents and it didn't have a hole in it, so her presents couldn't fall out of the bottom. Then Camilla put on a pair of clean, blue socks, and went downstairs for tea.

'Christmas shopping's boring,' said Camilla. 'We didn't buy anything for ME.'

'But Camilla,' said Mum. 'Christmas is for giving presents and gifts to other people. We buy presents for each other.'

'Why?' asked Camilla.

'Because at Christmas we remember that baby Jesus was born as God's wonderful present to us,' said Mum. 'And after Jesus had been born, wise men came and brought gifts to him.'

'What did they bring?' asked Camilla, nearly forgetting to grumble.

'They brought him precious gold, and special spices called frankincense and myrrh,' said Mum.

Camilla thought hard about that, then she said:

83

'Why don't we just buy what we want for ourselves?'
Mum laughed.

'There'd be no secrets or surprises then, would there, and when we give someone a present it's a way of saying that we love them and like them and want to share Christmas celebrations with them. We wouldn't be loving each other if we just bought things for ourselves.'

Camilla thought hard about that as well, and Mum said,

'Why don't you think of some Christmas presents that you could give, something special for Dad and Grandma and Grandpa and ... '

But Camilla had run upstairs to her bedroom, completely forgetting to grumble. There were one or two things she wanted to find.

The next day, Camilla and Mum went shopping again. And Camilla didn't grumble at all, not once, although they had to go by bus again because the car was still being mended. They went round the shops again, and Camilla, who discovered quite a lot of money in her money-box, bought all sorts of little presents. With a little help from Mum she bought notebooks and hankies and pens and pencils and chocolate Father Christmas shapes and lots of other things for Dad and Grandpa and Grandma and Aunty Debby and Uncle Gerald. She wrapped them up as soon as she was home again and wrote out everyone's names.

'I could make some presents, too,' said Camilla, whose bedroom was full of paper and glittery bits and material scraps and crayons and scissors and all sorts of bits and pieces. 'We make things at playschool. I'm making a – '

Then Camilla put her hand over her mouth because she'd remembered there was a secret inside it that mustn't pop out by mistake, and she wouldn't say any more.

Camilla was so busy that the days flew by until Christmas. She made Christmas cards for everyone and Mum helped her cook some biscuits. They should have been star-shaped but the cutter had mysteriously disappeared, then re-appeared a few days later.

A pile of little presents was growing in Camilla's bedroom.

'This is fun!' said Camilla.

'Present-giving can be fun after all,' smiled Mum.

'I suppose it can,' said Camilla, surprised. 'But where shall I put all my presents?'

Mum was busy sorting washing. She rescued one of Camilla's long, red socks from the wastepaper basket.

'Where's the other one?' said Mum, and Camilla slowly pulled it from under her pillow. She'd nearly forgotten!

'It was waiting for Father Christmas,' explained Camilla. Then she thought hard about all the gifts she'd made, and she said,

'That's where I could put all those presents! I can make a very big stocking for them all.'

Which is exactly what Camilla did. She filled the stretchy sock with all the little presents she'd made, until it was bulging and knobbly and ready to give to Dad and Grandpa and Grandma and Aunty Debby and Uncle Gerald on Christmas Day. Then Camilla crept into the airing cupboard one day and took the other red sock (the one with the hole) into her room for another surprise. But she didn't tell Mum.

On Christmas morning, Camilla remembered it was baby Jesus' birthday, and then she found a big pile of presents by her bed – in her rosebud-patterned pillowcase.

Christmas Day was wonderful and exciting and happy. There was church and carols and the twinkling lights on the Christmas tree and turkey and Christmas pudding and crackers and paper hats and candles. What a celebration, all for baby Jesus' birthday party, thought Camilla happily. Then there were more presents – and soon it was time for Camilla to give out her gifts from the long, red, stretchy sock.

'Oh Camilla, THANK YOU!' said Dad and Grandpa and Grandma and Aunty Debby and Uncle Gerald, and when Camilla had given out the last present, they all clapped her loudly, which made her feel very happy indeed.

'Oh, I nearly forgot,' said Camilla, jumping up and running over to the Christmas tree. She handed Mum the other red sock, tied up with red ribbon with an extra bow to cover the hole. Mum undid it carefully, and inside was a beautiful calendar.

It sparkled with glitter and was decorated with perfectly shaped coloured stars, very neatly cut out.

'That's funny,' said Mum. 'Those stars are exactly the same size as my biscuit cutter!'

'I made it at playschool,' said Camilla proudly. Although her gifts weren't like the special ones the wise men gave to the baby Jesus, giving presents had been fun after all.

Happy Birthday, Jesus, remembered Camilla.

PRAYER

Thank you God, for giving us Jesus on the first Christmas Day, and for the wise men who gave presents to the baby Jesus. Teach us all to share and to love and to give, because you first loved us. *Amen*

P O E M

Music

Thank you, God, for music;
For tinkly piano notes;
Tubas, horns and violins,
Guitars and pipes and flutes.

Thank you, God, for music
That makes us clap our hands;
Noisy, jazzy instruments,
Big orchestras and bands.

Thank you, God, for music
That makes us dance again;
Roundabouts and fairgrounds
And hurdy-gurdy men.

Thank you, God, for music
From birds high in the trees;
Water's gentle ripples,
Mighty roaring seas.

Thank you, God, for music,
For voices that can sing
Songs of praise and happiness;
Our thanks for everything.

Children all over the world enjoy music. In some other countries they sing different songs and play different instruments from the ones that we're used to. Ask your teacher or look in a book to find out what some of them are.

Yellow wellies

It was winter. There had been rain and wind and storms. Toby's mum had bought him new rubber boots because his feet had grown. The boots were yellow, and Toby was very proud of them.

'I like my yellow wellies,' said Toby. 'They're new and shiny and bright, and they've got nice patterns underneath their feet.'

Toby wore his new, yellow wellies all the time. He wore them upstairs and downstairs. He wore them in the kitchen and the living room. He wore them in the bedroom and the bathroom. Sometimes he wore them in the garden or to take Hornbeam, the dog, for a walk with Mum or Dad – but only when the sun was shining and the ground was dry. If it was raining Toby always put on his old wellies that were tight and very nearly worn out.

'I like my old boots best when it's raining,' Toby explained to Mum and Dad. 'The new ones will get wet! Then they won't be new any more.'

Early one chilly morning Dad said to Toby,

'Wake up! We're going out in the car today for a winter surprise.'

Toby liked surprises, especially if it meant going in the car. But he couldn't think what the surprise could possibly be. It wasn't anyone's birthday, and Christmas had happened already. Then Mum bundled him into all his warmest clothes – his thick jumper and his anorak and his scarf and his gloves and his woolly hat.

'And you'll need your boots,' said Mum.

Toby quickly found his old boots and put them on, while Mum and Dad piled all sorts of things under a rug in the back of the car. Then they set off, Hornbeam, the dog, as well.

Toby wondered what the surprise could possibly be. They drove through the town, round a roundabout, through some traffic lights, then out into the country-side with fields and farms. And then, after a lot more driving, they came to some flat marshes and a river – and then ...

'Seaside!' shouted Toby. 'I've just seen the sea!'

'That's our surprise,' said Dad.

'But we go to the sea in the summer,' said Toby. 'The seaside doesn't happen in the winter.'

'Oh, yes it does,' laughed Dad. 'It's good for fishing and exploring and birdwatching in winter. We're going to have a winter picnic.'

'But we have picnics in the summer,' said Toby. 'Picnics don't happen in the winter.'

'Oh, yes they do,' said Mum. 'If you eat outdoors – it's a picnic.'

Dad parked the car near the beach and Toby felt very excited. This was a very big surprise! Out of the back of the car came Dad's fishing tackle and an umbrella and Mum and Dad's boots and some extra anoraks and a ball and a big basket of picnic and ...

'My bucket and spade!' shouted Toby. That seemed

really strange.

The car park and the beach were almost empty. The sea looked rough and grey. Toby ran about all over the beach in his old wellies, and Hornbeam chased after him. They built a sandcastle, and made a lot of footprints in the sand. Hornbeam's feet made better prints because the soles of Toby's old wellies were flat and worn out. Then Toby noticed something round bobbing about in the water. He stood still, wondering what it was.

'Come on, we'll have to keep moving,' said Dad. 'There's a cold wind blowing.'

'The beach is different in the winter,' said Toby. 'It's all empty. There aren't lots of people or deckchairs and no one's swimming or eating ice-cream.'

'I should think not!' laughed Mum, wrapping her scarf against the wind.

'Do you feel like a swim, Toby?' teased Dad.

'NO!' said Toby. 'It's much too cold!'

'You can paddle, though,' said Mum. 'You've got your boots on.'

'Oh yes!' said Toby, looking longingly at the water. 'Come on, Hornbeam!'

Then, just as Hornbeam said 'Woof!', Toby said,

'Ouch! There's something in my boot!'

He tugged at his boot – and out flew a lot of sand, a pebble and a tiny shell.

'Oh dear,' said Mum. 'Your old boots have sprung a leak!'

It was true. One of the nearly worn-out boots had a hole in it now.

'That's from the pebbles,' said Mum, poking her finger through the hole.

'But I can't paddle!' wailed Toby.

'Indeed not,' said Dad, looking very serious, but with a twinkle in his eye. Then he went to the car and came back a few minutes later with ...

'My NEW boots!' shouted Toby. 'My yellow wellies! They were hiding in the car all the time – and I think they'd like to get wet today.'

Toby paddled in the sea in his new, yellow wellies. He splashed about in the waves. Then something came floating towards him.

'It's that round thing!' said Toby. 'It's all hairy! It's a – '

'Good gracious,' said Mum. 'It's a coconut! It's probably been washed up from a boat.'

'It may have drifted a long way,' said Dad. 'All the way from another country maybe, or it might have fallen from a boat.'

Toby was able to splash in his boots and reach the coconut. That was something VERY special to take home and show his friends!

Then Mum and Dad and Toby perched on some dry rocks and Toby looked across the cold, wintery beach while he drank soup from a thermos and shared a sandwich with some squabbling, hungry seagulls.

After the picnic, Dad went fishing for a little while at the harbour. Then they all took Hornbeam for a walk along the beach.

'These boots make good patterns,' said Toby, admiring his footmarks.

Higher up the beach was a line of shells and seaweed and cuttlefish and driftwood washed up by the tide, and all sorts of rubbish – orange peel and glass and a sock and plastic cups and squeezy bottles – even an old shoe!

'But how does it all get here?' said Toby.

'In the autumn and winter there are lots of storms and high winds,' said Dad. 'Remember the storm the other night? When the sea gets very rough the seaweed and bits of wood or rubbish from ships and boats are all tossed up by the tide.

'Like my coconut,' said Toby. 'Brr – I'm freezing.'

The wind whipped up big, white tops to the waves. Then Toby said,

'Look – it's snowing!'

Little, hard, white flakes were beginning to blow along the beach.

'But it doesn't snow at the seaside!' said Toby.

'Oh, yes it does sometimes,' said Dad. 'And it is!'

'Time to go home,' said Mum. 'It's freezing, and it will soon be dark.'

Toby took home a long piece of seaweed and some shells and the coconut. He nearly fell asleep in the car. But he stayed awake enough to say, 'I'm glad I wore my yellow wellies. They're good sea boots. And I like the seaside in winter. It's interesting.'

When they got home there was another surprise. Dad had caught four fish, and Toby and Dad and Mum had one each for supper. So did Hornbeam!

PRAYER

The seaside is such an interesting place, God, and in the winter it's so different. There's more and more to learn about every day in your exciting world. I'm glad I live in it! *Amen*

Other stories suitable for reading aloud to under 6s:

Tingling Tums
Margaret Barfield
Meet Dannielle, who discovers she can see in the dark;
Sam, who learns to ride a bike;

Jamie, who finds a big surprise waiting at his new home ...

Enjoy sharing the adventures of these and many other children featured in this lively new collection of contemporary short stories and poems.

Oliver and the Big Green Snake
Jan Godfrey
'Is that you, Oliver?' called Mum.

Oliver didn't answer. He was looking for a very good hidey-hole for his snowman.

'Come on, snowman,' said Oliver. 'You're going to hide in the food cupboard. You can eat a biscuit if you like.'

A humorous collection of short stories about Oliver, who is almost five. Oliver likes talking to things, especially his teddy bear, Bruin, but his talks with these imaginary friends often get him into trouble. His real friends Polly and Vimal and Honey the dog also feature in the stories.

Little Ted Lost
Mary Howard
At half-past seven it was time for bed. After he'd had his bath, put on his Fireman Sam pyjamas and cleaned

his teeth, Simon dashed into his bedroom and jumped on the bed. He looked under his duvet and under his pillow but his teddy wasn't there. 'Where is he, Granny? Where's my Little Ted?'

A collection of short stories and poems about Simon, his family, friends and Little Ted. Simon is four at the beginning of the book, but becomes five and starts school during the time covered by the stories.

Zac and the Multi-coloured Spidajig
Kathleen Crawford
'Yummy!' thought Sophie, 'they look delicious.'
  She was just opening her mouth and putting out her tongue to eat the first strawberry when it happened.
  'HIC,' went Sophie, and she shot high into the air, completely missing the strawberry she wanted to eat.

Meet Sophie, the frog with hiccups, Zac and his monster spider called Spidajig and Mrs McMuddle, who goes to buy a loaf of tomato soup.

A book of lively short stories, poems and simple prayers.

Bellowing Bartimaeus
Margaret Barfield

Pancake Fingers
Ro Willoughby

All these titles, except Tingling Tums, are also available as story cassettes from Scripture Union.